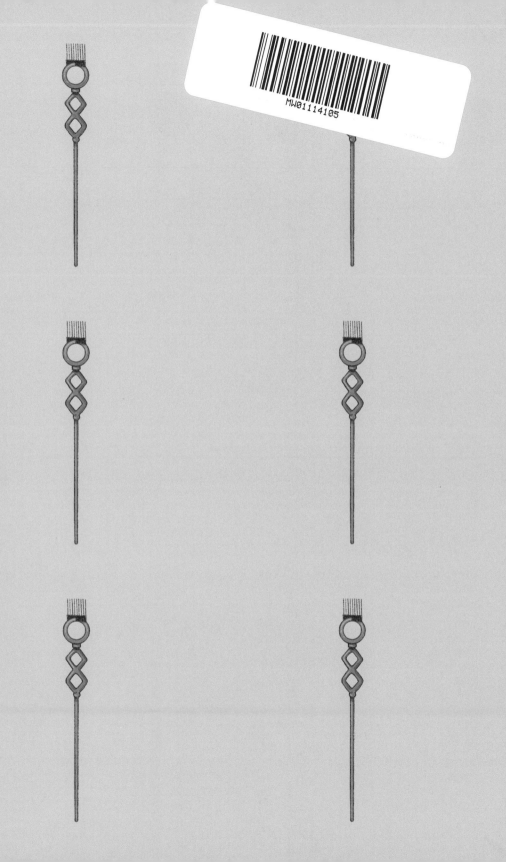

JUNIORS READ PUBLISHING

An imprint of Juniors Read LLC

To the people who could fly.

For inquiries, contact Juniors Read Publishing at *info@juniorsread.com*.

Illustrations by *Guy Wolek*

Cover Design by *Luis Pinto*

Graphic Design and Layout by *Russ Atkinson*

Creative Consultants: *Mindy, Olivia, Vivian, Miriam, and Isaiah Anderson*

Library of Congress Control Number: 2019937424
ISBN: 978-0-9990162-4-4
1 3 5 7 9 10 8 6 4 2

First Edition

Printed in China

VISIT

www.juniorsread.com

EMPRESS in the PLACE

I am Annie.

Izzie, that's me!

'Zinga, we're three!

by Donnie Mustardseed

Behold she holds
Strength in her hand.
As good as gold,
Her dark brown tan.

The sky is land.
The clouds are sand.
And she rules all
In this great land.

"A mighty sight
That's up on high!

8

"It is the Empress
In the sky!"

9

"There is no leader
Who's more wise
From where she rules
Above the skies.

"She is the best
In all she tries.
She is the best
Empress who flies."

12

"I am the Empress
In the sky.
A mighty sight
That's up on high!
And to succeed
High in the sky,
You must . . .
You have to . . .
Fly, fly, fly!"

"A mighty sight
 That's up on high!
 It is the Empress
 In the sky.
 I will impress her yet,
 You see.
 But how will I,
 Just being me?"

14

"Today the Empress
Calls a race
Of all the flyers
In the place.
Now, all are called
To race this race.
So all the flyers,
Please make haste!"

"An Empress,
  She will take my place,
  But only if
  She wins the race.
  She will, indeed,
  Rule up on high
  All that she sees
  Up in the sky."

"The fastest flyer
   Rules the sky,
   So will you race
   And have a try?"

20

"I cannot win.
Why would I try
To take her place
Up in the sky?"

"Are you not fast?
Are you not wise?
Are you not strong
Up in the sky?
You are the fastest
In my eyes,
Besides the Empress
In the sky!

"Yes, you can win!
And, if you try,
You must . . .
You have to . . .
Fly, fly, fly!"

23

"Why don't you try
To win the race
To be the Empress
In the place?
If you don't try,
How will you know?
If you don't try,
How will you grow?
If you believe,
And then you try,
You can succeed
High in the sky."

24

"What if I try
   And fail, you see?
What if I try
   And don't succeed?
I really fear,
   I'll try and fail!
I really fear,
   I won't prevail!
I really fear,
   I don't believe!
I don't believe!
I don't believe!"

27

"It's clear that fear
Has no place here.
Not here.
Not there.
Not anywhere!
See here.
No fear!
Yes, that is clear!
So if you care,
Please do not fear!"

"Now why not you?
   And why not more?
   If you can fly,
   Then you can soar!
   So will you cry
   Or will you try?
   Please join the race
   Up in the sky.
   The sky is yours,
   Yes, after all.
   For you to rise,
   First you must fall."

"I will believe
And join the race,
And race the flyers
In the place.
Yes, I will try
To win the prize.
I must . . .
I have to . . .
Fly, fly, fly!"

"You must believe
You can achieve.
You must believe
You can succeed.
But first, in you,
You must believe.
So to believe
Is all you need."

"I do believe
  I can achieve.
  I do believe
  I can succeed.
  But first, in me,
  I must believe.
  So to believe
  Is all I need.

"To be the best,
I must not be,
Not anyone,
But me you see!"

"High in the sky,
  She flies for you.
  Hold up a fist!
  That's what you do.
  To help her out,
  Give her a cheer.
  Hold up a fist
  Right in the air.

"Yes, cheer her on.
   You see them there?
   So many fists
   There in the air."

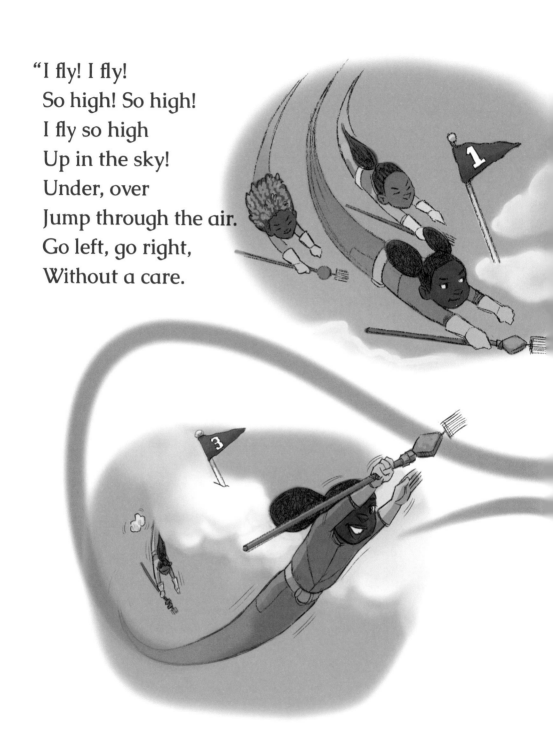

"I fly! I fly!
  So high! So high!
  I fly so high
  Up in the sky!
  Under, over
  Jump through the air.
  Go left, go right,
  Without a care.

"Up and forward,
Down, in between,

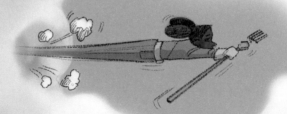

"I'm almost there,
Who would have seen?"

"Across, along,
In, out, behind,
Above, around,
Now first in line!

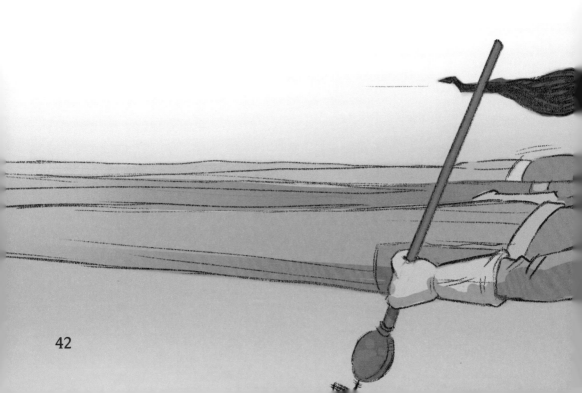

"I just might win,
    And win I might.
    You see, but not
    Without a fight."

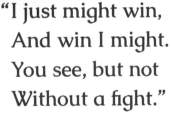

"She just might win,
    And win she might.
    She comes in first
    Just by a . . ."

". . . bite!"

"First in the race!
First in the race!
She is the Empress
In the place!

"First you believe,
Then you achieve!
So to succeed,
You first believe.
And to succeed
High in the sky,
You must . . .
You have to . . .
Fly, fly, fly!"

47

"There is no leader
    Who's more wise
    From where she rules
    Above the skies.

"She is the best
In all she tries.
She is the best
Empress who flies."

"Hear ye! Hear ye!
My first decree:
My sister,
She will rule with me,
Right by my side.
It is to be!
We two will rule
Together here.
See, not as one,
But as a pair!"

A mighty sight
That's up on high.
Up high above,
They rule the sky.

Behold they hold
Strength in their hands.
As good as gold,
Their dark brown tans.
The sky is land.
The clouds are sand.
And they rule all
In this great land. . .

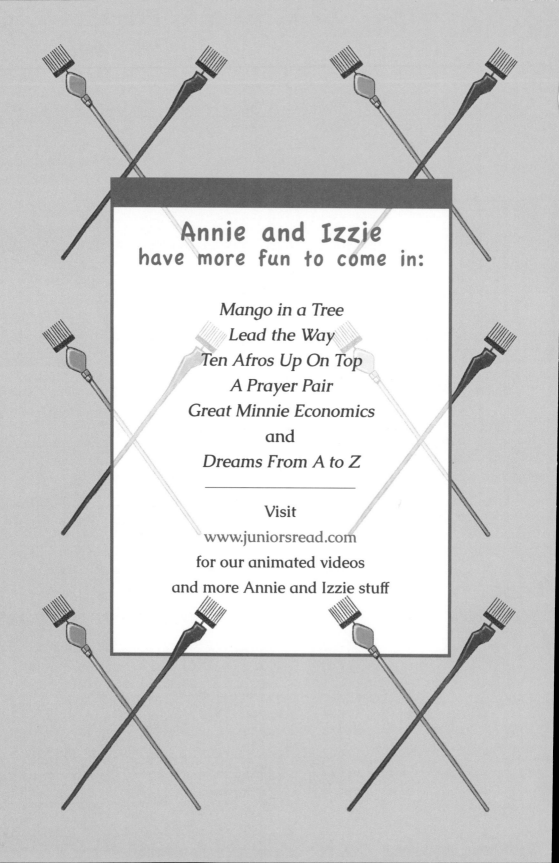

Annie and Izzie
have more fun to come in:

Mango in a Tree
Lead the Way
Ten Afros Up On Top
A Prayer Pair
Great Minnie Economics
and
Dreams From A to Z

Visit
www.juniorsread.com
for our animated videos
and more Annie and Izzie stuff